ANABAS

ANABAS

NON RESIDENCE

Soma Amrit Bhabani

ISBN:	Softcover	978-1-4828-4180-0
	eBook	978-1-4828-4179-4

The characters, the incidences, the locations, the talks used in this fiction novel anabas (non residence) are totally imaginary.

Any similarity of the said parameters with real one is a mere coincidence.

To order additional copies of this book, contact
Partridge India
000 800 10062 62
orders.india@partridgepublishing.com

www.partridgepublishing.com/india

Contents

Dedication

As it is the play of light
As it is the play of colour
As it is the play of bright and dark,

I must dedicate this fiction novel 'ANABAS 'to one my school teacher who saved me to be blind, living with light and colour.

In every respect, this book is the fruit of her good will, always with me.

--- Soma Amrit Bhabani ---

Acknowledgement

FIRST OF ALL, I MUST ACKNOWLEDGE THE GOD, UNLESS HIS BLESSING, THIS JOB WAS NOT POSSIBLE FOR ME.

SECONDLY, I AM THE MOST GRATEFUL TO THE PATRIDGE PUBLISHING LIMTED. WITHOUT THEIR CONSTANT INSPIRATION, COOPERATION AND GUIDANCE, I CAN NOT BE THE ACHIEVER.

AND ABOVE ALL, I MUST CONVEY MY THANKS TO THE MANY FRIENDS OF MY CITY AND OUTSIDE, WHO HAS ENCOURAGED AND HELP ME TO PUBLISH MY WORK.

AND ALSO, MY ADVANCE 'DHANYABAD 'TO THE READERS AND CRITICS FOR SPENDING SOME TIME FOR THE SAKE OF THIS 'ANABAS' (NON RESIDENCE) STORY.

--SOMA AMRIT BHABANI --

Preface

ANABAS (Non residence) is a value added fiction novel.

It is unique for world literature –a high tech space colony story.

The incidents, scenario, dress, and gadgets are all based on scientific theory. Many are well established, some under the research work of the author.

Anabas is a wrap type fiction novel. The space adventure to a satellite of Jupiter named Neo covers a fantasy, which is a classical physics love story. Here, the time of the two part of the story are different. The space expedition is a space tour of some grown up boys at 2500 A.D. and the fantasy is of 2100 A.D.

Anabas is the fifth fiction of the author's space colony sequel, starting from 'Antariksha 'followed by 'Amrit' and 'Abhijan'. And a twin of 'Abastav'. For that, some terms are in continuation from the previous. But those will not hamper the flow of the story.

As, Anabas is written for those of any age, having knowledge of science from senior school to Nobel laureate, having a passion for science and technology, the heavy dictionary words are not included and written in very simple

English language, easy understandable for those also whose mother tongue or schooling is not in English.

The author expects comments and criticism from the readers.

Soma Amrit Bhabani

Chapter one fanta(stic)she – 1

G M L

These letters! what these mean? Gladilova with the gift at her hand.

The chain with the pendant. A gift from Sumansuvra. Before leaving the earth Sumansuvra gift her.

A white crystal sphere with the three letters studded. Actually the buttons.

Gladilova push the M button unconsciously.

The orange jet fill the sky over the spice farm of Gladilova. Converging towards the horizon. Through the smog.

The farm members found Gladi nowhere within the farm. Not within the bunglow.

Chapter two fantashe – 2

The flash back (Abastav – Sur Real)---------------

Sumansuvra and Gladilova are the hero and heroine of this fantasy.

They are residential of two different planets.

The 'year' of these two planets are different, and the age of the citizens.

Gladilova live on Earth which rotates in that manner that one month is equal to twelve year of the planet of Sumansuvra.

When they meet on scope, Sumansuvra is of twenty and Gladilova is of thirty one.

By the blessing of God, Sumansuvra reach on earth, with the time inertia.

His age will increase as per his planet. He was allowed to stay with Gladilova for one month.

Gladi and Sumansuvra spent the time at a spice garden owned by Gladi at the lap of hills.

The day of romance end after one month. Sumansuvra had to return to his home leaving gladi.

Sumansuvra gift her the necklace – chain with the pendant.

Chapter three fantashe – 3

Memory. Gladilova was walking on memory.

Sumansuvra has left for few days. The days, the dream days, now a dream to Gladilova.

And now the days become intolerable. The strong loneliness.

Gladi, had live a life, a long life alone. She was habituated to live alone, to stay alone, to eat alone, to work alone, to walk alone.

Only within these thirty days, her habit has changed. Changed to live with other one.

The farm workers are waiting for her. It is the city apartment, at a distance from their farm. Sumansuvra bought it for their business purpose. Gladilova has no energy to move to the farm. Even not to take her breakfast.

Her farm is a very costly farm. Full of spice trees – different species.

Very sensitive, care requires for their growth.

Sumansuvra and Gladi, keep watch over each of them. Water, pesticides, fertilisers – they take the reports from the workers.

Gladilova spent a very simple life. But sumansuvra wanted gladi must be a special one. But when he is not here, why Gladi will walk on that road. Why now she will be there? Alone.

The logical fight ends. Liability win. Gladi gets up. Dressed and move to the farm.

After taking a round, she leave the farm to the workers – for the daily routine, went to the side of the pool, to her garden chair.

And enter to the memory. With the gift at her hand.

G M L.

Gladi my love

Gladi smiles. She find it. The meaning of the three letters.

Unconsciously, she pushed the letter M.

And vanishes.

Chapter four Neo

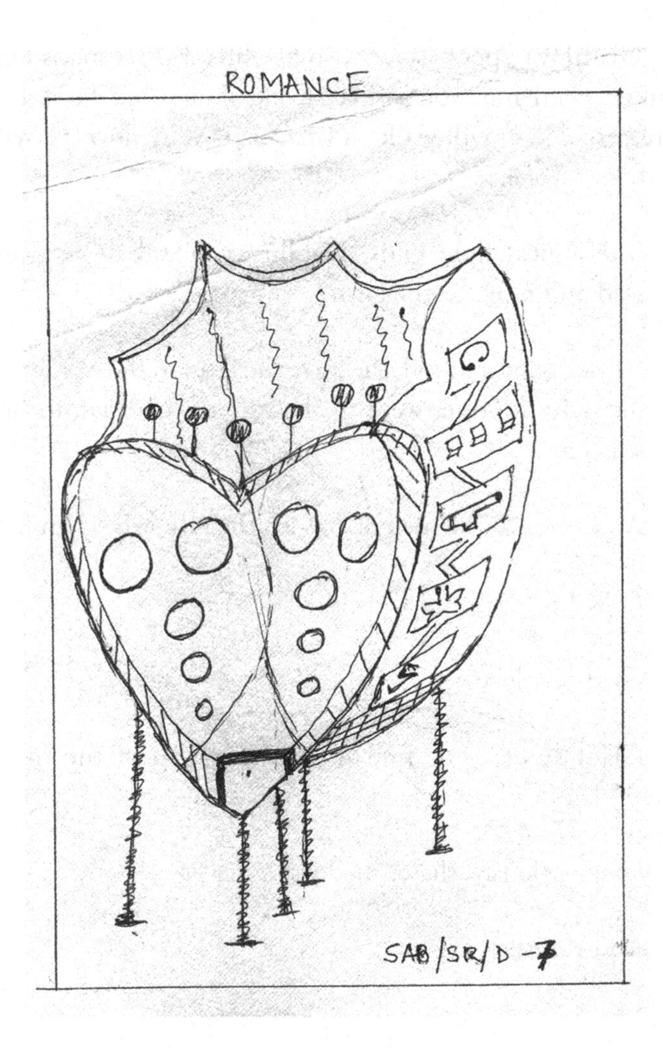

Infinity to the power of love – a break within the fantasy by Sou.

Bou has a habit to talk with mathematical notation.

All laugh to his words.

Correct – Pau supports. Now the space is powered by love.

After the face to face cold war between the Romance and the Hole seller group where the Romance group won, some days have passed.

The 'intelligent' short range missile destroyed Dingi – the space vehicle of the hole seller group.

Within these days, Romance – the special space vehicle of the young members of Iio has made a tour to Iio. Romance is specially made for their space expedition.

Iio people was worried about the hole seller group. They called Sou for some discussions. Sou, Kou, Pou, Nou all take a vacation from their research.

Sou Pou meet the Iio administrators. During return, Bou joined them.

Within their vacation, we must recapitulate some key words (from Abastav).

Once will be the time.

2500 a.d.

A satellite of Jupiter.
Mass is almost same as Earth.
Without any atmosphere.
Have no rotational motion along its own axis.

Iio

Another satellite of Jupiter
Mass much less than Earth.
The first space colony for human being.

Romance group

Romance is a high tech space vehicle for the Iio boys -
Young members of Iio. Space research workers.
Sou - team leader
Nou Hou Tou – junior members
Pou Mou Kou ----senior members
Fou – the biobot- a robot that takes organic foods

Sampan group

A teenager crossing boys' group - Aayna, Bayna, Khayna, Jayna from the Earth for research on Neo. Sampan is their space vehicle.

The stage

Neo is now moving from the winter to summer – the six month change.

Romance and sampan has landed this time over a white sand land.

At the center of that desert, there is a girl stone statue who is Uki, seated over a high cave base.

Last time, it was found,the base of Uki, a cave type, is filled with gas – a heavy inorganic at the lower and a light organic at the upper level.

Chapter five Orange jet

Yes, this time the infinity will be filled with love – Sou connect to the story.

After that war and vacation, the Romance group and Sampan group settled their protocols to stay at the white desert of Neo peacefully.

After long days, Sou returns to the diner time story for the Romance group. With the second part of the love story of Sumansuvra and Gladilova.

How? – Hou asked. How the space will be filled with love.

By the buttons M and L - my love.

No, actually the G is wrong. It will be T. M L T – the physical standards – Bou is always with the theory. Mass Length and Time

No, it is Gladilova – Nou want romance, not the physics.

Sou comments nothing. Romance group know, explanations will come at the last scene.

Romance group left Gladilova and the story vanishing.

Today i.e. tonight their interest goes to the secret of the buttons.

Buttons attached to the crystal.

Secret lies within the letters.

The buttons give Gladilova the wings. And wings to the fantasy also.

Chapter six fantashe – 4

Gladi is totally puzzled.

She is viewing a cinema for last one hour. Where she is the only character.

She is viewing her.

For last one hour, that Gladi is on a tour. One above atmosphere tour.

She was flying over the clove trees. Of her farm. Over the boundary Eucalyptus. Over the heads of Max, Bohr, Mary – the garden supervisors.

She is almost to touch the peak of the Eucalyptus. But she is going up and up.

Exponentially –

Bou interrupts Sou.

Max – spraying pesticide, Bohr – spraying water and Mary, who was sweeping the garden turns to small dots ; Sou ignores Bou.

Why exponential? It must be circular – Nou make objection whispering. The fight of brilliancy always goes on. Sou again ignore Nou.

Gladi views the cinema sitting at her armchair beside the swimming pool, where she was one hour latter.

She returns from a point, a far from her farm, over a barren land. Flying within the white clouds she returns to her farm. As like she woke up from a deep sleep. Max is approaching her with some questions. The first one is – where was she? Gladi mention the place down the hills. She knows they will not visit there leaving the works. Max shift the conversation to the pesticides.

Mary is now sweeping the road.

There is no trace of the orange jet.

Chapter seven — white desert

This time Santa will swim
By chariot aeromarine,

His sledge over the ice
Water beneath.

The stars kiss the earth
Shower blessing -
Sparkle over the ice.

Fau is at the front of Uki. Dancing.

Romance and Sampan boys are at the party. With Fau. With Uki.

Over the white desert.

Nou asked Aayna – have you sent the list of gifts?

The games the apps
The dongles the ring bell

Aayna gives lips to an old Christmas song.

Sou, joins with his elderly untuned voice

Merry
With the cakes
With the friends

The battle is over few days ago. Before the starting of their daily routines, one get together was must.

The twelve hour twelve hour duty of two groups has started. Neo has no day and night. The watch – atomic watch keep the day and night.

The bed time story has returned to the Romance boys.

Both the groups have collected the upper and lower layer gases from the base of Uki. Both the group are analysing those.

Rona has left the sampan group. For his marriage. Bayna is only of the Sampan group who is not happy.

Uki has cheated him. No, not Uki actually. It is Sou. Sou won this love battle. Sou was the soldier of Fou.

And that CADberry wins. (the biobot is a computer aided device with berry software).

Bayna, not enjoying the party, concentrate to the gazettes brought by Sou during their last visit to Iio.

He pass Khayna - concentrating to the delicious come with Bou.

Bou! a new problem. There was only Sou enough for his team, another one.

The gas is of no interest of him. There must be something more to Uki.

Something very precious.

Chapter eight Fantashe – 5

After taking a long sun bath at her garden chair, Gladi concentrate to her work.

Take the report from Max and Bohr.

The clove trees are rapidly grow up. Flowers are just to come.

Max tell her that the Cardamoms are facing some problems.

Gladi moves to the trees. Her hang over has over.

On one side of the farm, the nursery is made. Some fertilizers are poured over the leaves of the baby Cardamoms. Gladi felt anger. These are very costly plants. Advice the workers to do work cautiously. Gently. And sympathetically.

Bohr is the expert of Botany. He shows the workers what they have to do. Cutting of some leaves. Spraying water to the others.

Max is examining the little Saffron. They are just got birth.

With the Sunset, Gladi returns to her farm cottage. Two or three days she will stay here and then will return to their city apartment.

Gladi took her food. She is again alone at the dining table.

Putting the dessert for late night, Gladi with the gift from Sumansuvra sat in front of the twinkling sky at the balcony. This is her favourite place of this Bunglow.

The necklace with the pendant. A white crystal. G M L three letters of gold engraved.

That time she had pushed the letter M. Yes, her memory nods. And once. Only once.

This time, Gladi, consciously push the M button. Twice. Counting within mind.

The balcony becomes vacant.

Only Mary, who was out of her quarter, at the grass, with her grandson, found a yellow jet within the dark. Like some fire works.

At very far, on the other part of the world, where that was the day time, some office goers found a yellow smoke jet at the blue sky with the white cloud groups. Though, no sign of any air ship was found.

It was like someone spread the petals of yellow roses over the blue bed.

Chapter nine Romance

Spirit ---- Pou found it.

The organic part of the gas is Spirit, he announces.

From the cave type base part of the girl statue, a very small amount of gas comes out. Through some natural pores within the stones.

The Romance boys found that from the upper part of the cave the light organic gas and from the near ground part a heavy inorganic gas are out.

They were trying to get the nature of the gas, after collection.

This is the night of the Romance. They are at the diner table. The juniors are in between the fantasy.

Spirit – Nou whisper, Gladi has the spirit.
How? Hou ask.
She is living alone, without Sumansuvra, directing her farm – Nou gives the lesson.
Spirit of true love – Tou almost in mute.

The juniors concentrate to their special menu.

But, you can not collect a amount, the pores are fine –Pou comments.

That is of no use of us – Sou supports Pou's thought.

We have to find some way – Pou make the task.

Gladi must find some way – Tou, beside Gladi.

And she will find – Bou is optimist.

Why? why you are so sure? – Nou, always opposing Bou.

As God loves vectors, not the scalars, and Gladi has a vector love – Bou mathematically solve the problem.

Why God loves vectors? – Hou tries to understand. He needs some time for these critical Maths.

For scalars, there is a probability to get the final result a zero – Bou

As for example? – Nou

Suppose you are not walking in straight line, rather over a circle – Bou put it.

The net work done is zero – Bou with a victrious smile, and you see victory and vector are almost synonymous, he ends.

So, Gladi must fly in one direction, like her love – Tou calculates.

Obviously, and with counting the mileage per button press – Bou, trying to give flow to the fantasy.

There are two more buttons – Kou joined them after finishing his dish.

Chapter ten Sampan

Third bracket MUST COME second bracket first bracket YOU plus KHAYNA first bracket close TO OUR CAMP second bracket close third bracket close --- Bou to Bayna.

Bayna dislikes Bou for his way of speaking.

Oh yes plus first bracket AT 8 PM first bracket close – Bou adds.

Bayna understand. Invitation to Romance. This must be a new game for them. Fu h h

Bou is boring and huky puky. Very difficult to understand his words and the weight. Bayna has within his memory – the first meeting

Where is 'Bayna bar'? – Bou asked that day. He was alone working within sampan. Others were at the field.

Bayna asked the meaning of the words. The complement, the complement of your set,

Bayna understand. Bou was asking about the other members of Sampan.

Bayna nod to the invitation and make a bye to Bou. He has many thing to do now.

At the battle, Romance has proved their improvement, their technology, the self controlled gazettes – gazettes with eyes.

Bayna is now running after those. Trying to get the circuits. But it needs more knowledge and experience. He has informed the authority at Earth.

He spends his full day for the gazettes. At sampan evening, Aayna Khayna Jayna back from their work.

Khayna quickly prepare their food. Simple their home type. at the diner time, Bayna makes light the environment with the Bou words.

Aayna quickly catch and return the ball – then today's fresh news is Gayna bar bar is coming.

All are happy. Gayna, though quite angry type but simple and jolly. Arms specialist. He must be with many stories from their home land.

Why bar bar? Khayna asked. Gayna is just coming first time. Barbar in Bengali means many times.

Not in Bengali, and also not in English, it is the mathematics language, Aayna answer him in his bass voice.

Chapter eleven — Fantashe – 6

Chocolate - Gladi smile. A big chocolate. Gladi verify this side and that side of that.

The chocolate has resided within her refrigerator for last few months, Till Sumansuvra leaves her. She kept it like a jewel of her jewellery box. A gift from her fiancé.

Gladi is not very fond of chocolate. But Sumansuvra likes to gift it. He likes the dry fruits. To consume them in several means.

Last five days she was at her city apartment. Busy with her business. Today she reaches her farm. After launch, now she will join the farm workers.

She engage Mari to clean the rooms of the bunglow. And come downstairs, at the garden. Max and Bohr are there. Instructing the workers. She found max with water vista, Bohr is not at sight.

Sumansuvra's regular gift was the chocolates. From the very beginning. That time they were at the beach resort. Gladi reminds how Sumansuvra felt shy to present the gifts.

News from max. No, all are well.

That time, the age difference, was the prominent point. And also the background.

The flowers of Cardamom are being dry. Changing their colours.

The Saffron are seem ill to Gladi. She waits for Bohr. He is the doctor. Specialist of these diseases. That will be great loss if these plants die.

Those days were the lazy days, not like now. She has to remain alert all the time about her works now. This week she went to the city to sell the leaves of the eucalyptus. To some medicine makers.

Gladi was a simple girl. Living daily life. To some extent fool, according to Sumansuvra. This new life is the best gift from him.

Before her exit from the bunglow, Gladi kept the chocolate again to her fridge.

With the Sunset, Gladi, sits at her armchair beside the pool. She is now with her memory.

Bohr, hearing from Max, with quick steps proceed for Gladi. To report about his absence.

Bohr, keep the report for the time being. He found Gladi in deep thought.

And, a cherry red band of light has surrounded Gladi.

Chapter eleven (2) fantashe – 7

That time –

My heart

Becomes non resident

Sumansuvra is singing before the gift, gift from gladilova.

My heart becomes non resident

To get warm of home

Smansuvra change the scale

The selfish heart left me

Enters to non residence

Flies far

To get its life

Sumansuvra repeat the song and add

To listen the echo of its beats

Sumansuvra makes a pause, and then compose

To listen the echo of its beats

My heart is in resonance

Chapter twelve Romance

Laws of association – Bou is serious.

Nou Kou Tou are anxious. This type mathematical conversation is new to them.

Bou has just returned from Sampan.

With a news.

A new comer – name Gayna, one armoury expert, has joined sampan.

He is best friend of Aayna – Bou disclose the secret.

The Romance group was thinking about the cause. Matter is not so simple – Gayna is on a holiday visit. A new plan? They are thinking.

So, he is my best friend also. Bou teaches – by the law of association.

Huhh – Tou is disappointed. I t's not a matter of joke. Though the sampan group is now their friend. But the earth is not friend of Iio.

But, just now they leave the matter, for the seniors. Return to their discussion. The research.

Gas within Pharaoh's belly –Bou, always with easy solution, we shall push a pin there.

And all the gas will be out – Nou, teasing. Talkative fool – opinion about Bou, behind the stage.

They are talking about the girl stone statue – Uki, about its stone base. They had already tried to inject pin to hammer, but it is impossible.

And it is also not known that what will be the effect. If the gas, gases come out.

Whether the aromatic will be Camphor, at space – question has arose.

No – Bou speak.

No? How you are so sure? – Hou ask.

Not no, but NO, Nitrous Oxide – Bou explain.

Nou catch. Bou expects NO will form from the heavier nitrogen bad smell gas. The Ammoniacal.

Their day time approaches to the evening.

Nou show the watch, the necklace of Uki. The atomic watch.

It's evening, we have to leave now, Nou tell Bou.

Day time – evening - Bou dislikes these words.

No sign of Sunray, daytime, fuhh- his general expression.

But, today, there is Sunray! Just arrive.

Chapter thirteen Uki vanish

No Uki, Uki is not at her place! – Khayna rub his eyes.

He has just woke up. By reflex, he call other members of Sampan.

Gayna jump from his bed. Aayna tries to understand. Khayna has a habit to make chaos, he is afraid of many thing. Aayna take some time to react to Khayna. Jayna, one level up of Aayna, as usual pays no attention to Khayna. Bayna, after his personal tasks, take rest at late night, almost at the morning. Only, he goes on sleeping.

Gayna, quickly take his position, beside Khayna, at the window of Sampan. And make the echo – yes, no Uki, no Uki.

Noh.. today half an hour sleep is lost – Aayna get up. Jayna, still at bed. Where will go?

But, now, Bayna make a somersault, within his sleep, he heard that Sou has taken away Uki.

Uki vanishes! This time, Khayna is proper. He is not in want of a helper, to serve the morning tea.

But, here is no Hudini or P C Sirkar, to vanish Uki – Bayna, stunt.

He wish to walk to the center of the white desert. To verify the happenings.

Aayna hold him. Wait, let us think. There may be some danger. Some unknown fact. Of this space.

Not the space, must the Romance – words within Bayna's mind.

Then? - Gayna. He always fill up the pause by this word. His favourite.

We must not be out of Sampan, it may be due to the gas leak, or some other natural phenomena – Aayna is firm.

Others accept. Then? - Gayna want the alternate.

We shall contact Romance, Aayna suggest.

Huh.. they have make it, and we will go them – Bayna, against his mind. He knows Romance has not made any harm to them till now and Aayna will remind that.

Jayna has joined in between. He supports Aayna.

The romance boys are at the field now, it is their evening, all are at their work their.

Aayna contact Nou, works till last minute.

Now? Uki is here? – Nou answers, why? Obviously, we are in front of it. Fou is just beside.

Aayna ignore the anger of Bayna, hearing the news, specially of Fau.

Then? Gayna, with eyes outwards, no, Uki is not in view till now.

Aayna, contact Sou, the wise. And send the message.

When the Romance boys are there, there is no poison, nor magic.

Sampan boys get ready for the field.

Chapter fourteen fantashe – 8

What a 'family family' weather it was! Gladi is with her memory. At her farm bunglow. With the rain green sea at the retina.

That was the first day of the last week. They were in decoration of their apartment.

Gladi found at her mind screen, she was placing the curtains. They bought it from city mall matching with the wall colour of the rooms. Sumansuvra was helping. His height is the advantage.

The necklace – gift from Sumansuvra is at its place. The pendant attract her attention. Last two times she pressed the letter M of the pendant.

The time of flight. Gladi discover the difference. The second day she made a fly to a far. She was long time absent from her work. To Gladi, it is not a sleep nor a awake feeling. After return, she open her photo series.

That day they spent the day in those interior settings. A life separate from Gladi's single life. They place the dining table, after many discussion. And much more time then for the quality of the dining set and launch set. Those must not be same. If the lunch set is of clay, the diner set must be of glass.

And my milk set? And my juice set? Where will be the flower vas? Gladi can not think her rooms without flowers and without some aroma.

Sumansuvra placed Gladi's paintings here and there. They are very so so, but the recent works. The sea beach, the granite cut mountains, the strawberry garden, the village fair hang on the walls. Overcoming Gladi's negative attitude.

It was a good ride, a memorable. Gladi analyse. Now she is flying over so many places. With a very high velocity, still some scenes are in her mind. Somewhere, the ground was covered with sand – yellowish, somewhere it is white – totally snow spreading.

Sou is continuing his fantasy at bed time, for the Romance boys.

Gladi is thinking about her last ride. Probably I had pressed the L button.

A change of L shell – Bou got interested now.

Whose? Nou ask

How? Hou stand beside.

Gladi or Sumansuvra's – Bou give the answer.

L shells are for atoms – Tou remind them

Man is made of atoms – Bou, no defeat mood.

And for man, L shells are for love and M shell are for marriage – Bou explain.

I got it, Tou to others, those shells must be empty to get love

Or to be married – Kou quite disgusted. These are very light talks.

Sou, before enter to sleep, ends, today Gladi push the M button once and the L button twice.

Chapter fifteen — Nature's magic

What a sensational news – the sampan boys' run towards Romance.

Sou was at Romance, with the lab, with Kou, Mou.

Aayna Khayna knock the door, Sou open it, the boys' run to the window.

No..o..o.. Uki is still vanish, from romance also. Sou Kou follow them. They were busy with their duty. Others are at the field. They need not to look at Uki. If anything happen unusual, Nou Pou will inform Sou. But no news from there.

Sou connect Tou. Uki is as usual.

Then? - Gayna's question.

Sou take them out from Romance. Walk towards Uki.

After a distance, Uki comes to view. Somehow brighter than other days – seem to the team.

Sou, with the team move towards Sampan. And, like the previous, after a distance, Uki is invisible.

All are astonished. Except Fou. He is with Uki. These are not his cup of tea.

But how? Hou ask.

Mirage – Gayna, from memory.

Bayna get angry. No knowledge of science. Mirage require the atmosphere.

The team make a round. The desert is under the flood of light by the nuclear battery.

Sou found it. Uki and some near zone is dazzling. Making the zone total white.

Sun ray - Sou got the answer. It was within their calculation that one portion of Neo will be out from umbra and pen umbra soon.

The winter is gone – Romance group starts singing.

But, Sun rays vanish Uki? Bou, after a long silence. Physics is quite tough. He likes mathematics.

The scattering, the superposition. Over uki, the sunrays and the artificial light mixing, the dazzling forms. And the view becomes opaque to some area.

Not to Fou – Bayna is not happy, Fou is just at the base, the line of sight is different.

Sou ask Tou to off the lights.

It is spectacular. The soft sun light covers Uki. From the deep dark, they view it.

The autumn comes.

Chapter sixteen — Black book

With the cakes with the friends

Fau's feet is in salsa rhythm. After many days, the Romance group and the Sampan group is dancing.

The cake is for the celebration, celebration of the sunrise. After six month. Gayna is the new cook for the combined group.

Bayna is not with others. Today again a defeat. He is thinking. About this phenomena.

After the party, Romance group wish to take a trip at above. For many days, they did not make that. Sampan boys' are now on duty.

Ferry – their cab for flying. Single sitter space cab. For some days, those are left inactive. Sou advice to check the vehicles first.

The Romance boys' check instruments, and get ready to fly. The Sampan boys' do not possess any ferry type vehicle. Gayna wishes to fly with them. They agree asking Sou.

Nou Tou Kou make bye to Fou and start their cab. Pou demonstrates the steps of driving.

Black book - the Ferry data recorder, the fuel indicator ....

Gayna understand. Kou return to his vehicle. He makes the thumbs up. Gayna tries to start. Kou also.

Hou Tou were in delay. They find Kou and Gayna are also at the hanger.

With the friends with the cakes
They also start flying, with the song.

Sou and Fou return to Romance.

Kou check all the points. He is the best. Never face this type of problem.

Gayna is now at primary. He also tries from his just learned knowledge.

Then he call Kou. Kou, with the Gayna's, tries some time.

Suddenly, his brain strikes. He check the previous data, from the black book.

Not matched – error comes. The black book is not fitting with other instruments.

Kou got it. It's of his vehicle. Two were at his hand. And interchanged.

He change the black book and hand over the ferry to Gayna.

He does it consciously, within this time Gayna invented it. They are not liking this. Must be. Otherwise, at least Aayna will join.

Now he wants to back to his duty. Kou leave him. And start his spaceship.

Bou arrive to Gayna. He was with the Sampan. Flying is not his liking.

Second bracket start first bracket start 'I plus you' first bracket close 'will make some' second bracket close 'other thing'.

Gayna agree.

Chapter seventeen Uki black out

All the hair white! Khayna, being the early riser, found it. He put the tea kettle, and verify from the doors. Uki is at her place but with the white hairs.

Other sampan boys' were waiting for the tea. Jump up. These days are going amazing. The heavenly bodies are showing magic.

They found Uki, with fair complexion, but white hair. The light and shade show.

Due to the relative volume and speed of Jupiter and Neo, Neo remains six month at 24 hours night, now slowly it is entering to 24 hours day.

But, the position of Uki – Sou is thinking. After some time they will return to Romance evening. The position of Uki is interesting. The rotational effect of Neo is prominent here.

Like the Konark – Nou, they are returning now. You know Bou, the sun rays always fall on the face of Sun statue at Konark.

Bou nods. Today the faint sunray fall over the hairs of Uki. Bou look at a glance to Fau. Fau must be sorry, as Uki seems old today.

It will save a lot of power – Sou, with hope. We will try to generate the internal power also from the sun.

He already make some lighting arrangements off at the desert. For that, some portion of Uki goes to dark, with the sun ray scattered at head.

Fau was viewing the sky. Bou tries to understand what he is searching. Being unsuccessful, he ask Nou.

Gladi, he is searching Gladi. He heard with us that Gladi flies over our head being band of colour – Nou makes joke

Gladi is hanging – Bou, she had pressed the buttons, M button once and L button twice

Yes, for that, Bou is looking for orange band, at the sky, due to the L button twice, she is flying far and far – Nou explain seriously,

And may makes a visit to us – Bou

They call Fou. It's their evening tea time.

Chapter eighteen fantashe – 9

The red shari. The colour of the ray was like her that red shari. The ray bound her. As if, she was in that dress.

Gladi was seating at her garden chair. She was tired. spent a lot of hours for the agachha, these small plants, at the roots of the costly trees will damage them.

The red ray – the cherry red ray – cover her in many turns. And it reminds her the only red dress of her.

The red silk shari – once upon a time her father made a gift. She dislike to wear red. It never suits her. She kept the shari very carefully neatly at her custody. That's a gift for her 'once will be marriage'.

Bohr brings some books for her, from the city. Utility of the cloves. Uses of it. And how it can be preserved.

She will make the orders at night, when she will be at the bunglow. Alone. For the products of the cloves of her garden. Business. The word makes her laugh.

After her diner, which takes few minutes now, she chew two of her cloves. No, it's fine – strong, the juice make her throat clear.

She sat to calculate, the profit, whether she will sell the raw or the pharmaceutical products.

May be the profit large, but it will need man power and time. Better we can try for some thing new. They need not much money. For innovation, she starts to go through the books.

Playing with her necklace, which she keep at her hand when she is alone.

After few pages, she walk to her favourite place – the balcony. The whitish sky is above, the pool and trees and the lights of the staff quarters.

Sumansuvra collected the story, of the red shari. he wanted to see that. Gladi showed him.
Sumansuvra takes the place of the cloves. Gladi remains standing at the balcony.

She feels herself passionate, wishing to meet Sumansuvra just now.

Gladi, by excitement, press the L button four times and M button four times.

Must be hanging over Romance, I told you, Bou in continuation from the field.

That was twenty first century, five hundred years back, mind that – Sou makes stop him and continues,

Bohr was at his quarter balcony. He found an indigo bow, running towards the horizon.

This place is mystic, I must consult one climate expert, he thought.

Chapter nineteen Rambo

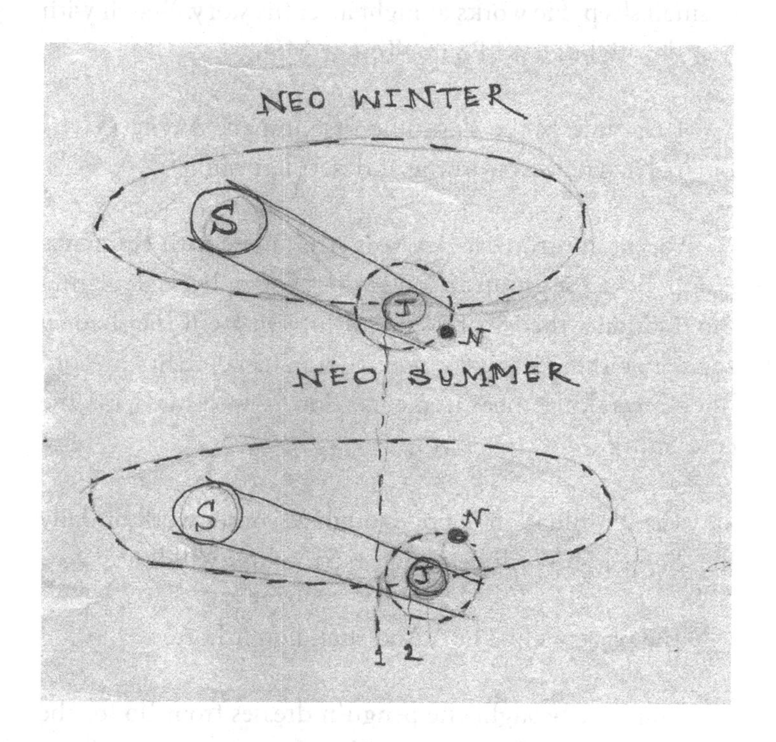

The summer.

Neo's season change has started. The cold is decreasing day by day.

Sou is taking his morning walk around the white stone statue Uki. She is now out of darkness. Neo's rotation now makes the white desert fill with soft sunray.

The desert is still a white desert.

Other romance boys' are still at bed. Sou is habituated of small sleep. He works at night after his story. Watch with that day night guard Pou or Tou or Mou.

That time is the day time of Sampan. Aayna Gayna Bayna Khayna was working at desert last night.

Sou has heard that Bayna is still angry with Romance group. Both the group are now with geography. Calculating the rotational theory of Neo and Jupiter, from the shadow zone. For the Sampans', now the artificial lights are off. They are taking measurements. Sou is walking with the cold Sunray.

The illumination is not enough for other work or daily life. Some lights will be on when Sampans' will leave.

The place will be hot. And then hotter hottest.

Romance brought the penguin dresses from Iio for the winter. Those will not work. They have to change those. Very soon.

Nou Kou Hou approaching Sou. With their chat. Nou deliver the secret to Sou – the earth people have sent a message to them. Them means the Sampan. Sou understand. Nou continues – Romance have made the – intelligent weapons, copying them.

Then, why they did not use it? When they are the creator! – Kou, join after his slow breakfast.

That's their point – Nou is medium excited, the idea was their, they could not finish before us. Nou, at his visit to Sampan with Bou got the conversation with the hole seller group. That was about the fight for black hole selling, between Romance and black hole black marketers.

Rambo – Sou smiles.

Others want to know about the word.

That is the code word for these type of expressions. False ego for a looser.

Hi hi … they laugh together. Let them be Rambo.

They will not leave us – the HS group – Pou,

Then Rambo 2 – Tou announces,

The series of war, like the great wars – Kou,

Series? A.P. or G.P.? – question from Bou.

Chapter twenty Fantashe – 10

May be A.P., may be G.P. – but Gladilova is in progression, towards the infinity, - Sou, now with his fantasy. She must find Sumansuvra, she must be at his side.

She can find Sumansuvra at his galaxy scope, but that only scene. With the spring breeze, the indigo band is spreading toward the vacuum.

But, the villains – Sou takes the u turn of his story.

It is new to the Romance boys. They have the real life villain – the HS group, but till now the fantasy had no villain.

You can take them as the witch, Sou makes the image clear. Some old known women of Gladilova – bad women. Jealous to her.

The earth people are alike – Nou comments.

No change on fourth dimension – Bou makes clear.

But these are witches of a classical love story, Pou reminds them, obey classical physics.

The witches here act classical – Sou add, not like general witches. The science fiction, have assumption, must not any witch. They divert the topic to science fiction.

The writers are not research scholars, they assume,not involve generally true science – Sou is wise.

These witches, have many gazettes, not only the nails or teeth, Sou continues.

Gladi had left her village for many days, but these witches keep contact with her, came to know about Sumansuvra and other many things.

And, obviously, they don't like those, the wealthy and prosper Gladi, they seek some way to turn her at the ground.

But, now she over the sky – Tou interrupts.

Above the sky, almost to escape, but, Sou take a pause, for the sake of the story.

The happiness – it is the most important matter, the witches can never tolerate happiness of other. Not only of Gladi, but of you,I.. Bou, after a long silence.

Gladi is happy for Sumansuvra, nothing else, Sou overtaking the comments, and the witches never recommend that.

Gladi was floating over the clear blue sky, flying, hopping ...,

A strong wind, a storm -Sou is sorry for Gladilova with others, for the defeat,

Gladi wake up from her sleep. The doors and windows are in harmonic motion.. for the wind.

Gladi run inside.

Chapter twenty one — Power station

Something divided by infinity-

Bou is at primary level of flying. Today is a holiday for Romance. The boys wish to fly.

Day to fly. Fly over the desert and a far. Within the twinkling stars. Which are seem very near, but actually a million light year distance.

A narrow lane is found through two small stars, like a partition of a single. Bou make the comment.

Zero – we know that, coach Nou answer.

No, two star – Bou straight his forefinger.

The ferry are in folk. Bou is examining the activities of each part. We need the fuel, Gladi is lucky, she need not, for her journey – Bou, with the fantasy. He is trying to solve the science behind. But, till no solution, and the fantasy become not appreciable, not acceptable to him.

Gladi has no vehicle, Pou response to Bou, they are making audio conference through the gazettes, but you know, once upon a time – the mythological era – there was one saint named Narod, who used to travel by a vehicle which need no fuel.

Narod – Tou makes the echo, and the vehicle?

A seesaw type, wooden, no gear, no accelerator, only the central stirring – Pou has depth in myth,

But how? – Hou is thinking.

By yoga, you can do anything by yoga – Pou has believe.

Anyway, we have our little power station, these are tiny nuclear battery – Nou is happy with ferry.

Today, they have the aim to visit a space station, a space power station, recently formed. The scientists there are for research to generate power from black holes. The gas evolved from the gas holes.

Mainly, the space crafts and stations are operated by sun ray, but sometimes they have to enter to dark zone for the heavenly bodies, their positions, the stations were facing power crisis. They now expect to overcome that.

The Romance boys fly nearer to station. The Earth people are working there. To place the station over one semi dead black hole.

Bou observe more seriously than other. The hot hole. The jet of heat energy will be utilised.

They take the turn. Towards Neo. Above the head of Romance.

Ferry are flying. With the birds' eye view.

Chapter twenty two — Uki lift up

4 cm
exactly 4 cm– Bayna take the measurement.

4 months have passed. From the day of first sun shine. The temperature is medium now. Neo has out of umbra, but till in the pen umbra. After some days, it will be completely free from Jupiter.

The penguin dress are returned to home. No penguin over the Iceland now. Romance and Sampan both team are now at normal space suit.

Uki is now out of eclipse. The Jupiter eclipse. A very special experience for the boys. Separate from their other space expedition. Iio people viewed it, but out of telescopic range for the earth.

Bayna is astonished, 4 cm! Something wrong. But, telescope reading can't tell lie. It is in ok condition.

The height of Uki is increased. Bayna leave Sampan and move to others, at the field. He check the traces over the white dust.

What you need to find? Gayna ask. In between time, he get the habit of Bayna.

Earth quake - Bayna's short answer,

Neo quake – Gayna makes the correction.

Bayna, with few words, gives the news.

Gaining height, at this age – Aayna makes the joke.

Has it increased step by step, day by day? Aayna ask Bayna, as telescope readings are under Bayna's responsibility.

No,suddenly – Bayna check all the related data about the desert in time interval.

The Sampan boys pass the day in meeting. To establish a fact about this natural phenomena.

It is not by the Romance, as the whole seat goes up, not any particular corner.

And no quake, as there is no crack anywhere over the desert.

Hopelessly, they returned to Sampan.

At diner, they got the message. From Sou. The gas within Uki's base is expanding – due to the temperature. May be slowly, but it is expanding.

Expanding! Then? The question is before all.

But, Bayna is happy. He got a new problem. Food to brain.

Chapter twenty three Fantashe –11

You are all surround
You are all around

Gladilova is walking on pebbles. She is walking through the garden. She is totally disappointed. She was.

She is singing. A song learnt from Sumansuvra. To make her fresh. She was disappointed. For the storm. The barrier came before her escape. Stand between Sumansuvra and Gladi.

Your breadth touch me
Your smell flows here

It will diffusion – Bou interrupts Sou, within the fantasy.

Sou system makes no handshake.
your breadth diffuses within my

Bou makes a new line of the song. He sings it with his own tone and notes. Irritating all. Even Nou – who generally likes the scientific talks. But this is a semi climax of the fantasy. No one is liking any changes just now. No loss of concentration – for the speaker or the audience.

come with the wind
    come with the wind
        come with the wind

Sou sings this line in opera style – in very high pitch. As Gladi is singing here.

and not with the storm – Pou makes a little joke.

Must not, storm is the villain, Gladi could not reach Sumansuvra – her beloved due to this storm.

Gladi now, just at this moment, want to hear Sumansuvra singing. She quickly back to her room, to her galaxy scope. Far far away from Gladi. But a clear view.

No, he is not singing. He is on his way. To somewhere. To some work. The view seems as he is approaching Gladi. As like few months ago. Gladi is at her bunglow balcony. Sumansuvra is returning. Through the lines of Eucalyptus trees over the pebble path.

the distance is now in light years.

Gladi's time is passing. With Sumansuvra walking.

Max makes a break. He has to report something.

Max is well – Bou add.

Why? Tou ask. It is not he likes.

As, he is Maxwell. Otherwise, Gladi will forgot her works. Her daily routine - joke from Bou.

Yes, Gladi talk with Max. Then she returns to her world. Made of Gladi and Sumansuvra.

But now, there is no trace of Sumansuvra over the screen. Gladi makes a search. But, no,there is a technical problem.

Gladi with her memories sit at the balcony. With the reddish ray surrounding. As like from the street light. The spring wind touches her. Touches her hairs, her lips. Gladi get drowned within the breeze.

Chapter twenty four Cheater never prosper

But problem lies – Sou whisper. The self guided gazettes.

Sometimes past, Sou was in describing Gladi. The heroine of the fantasy. Gladi, that day, were a special dress. A sleeveless top with a long skirt. With floral print. With a special hat. Favourite of Sumansuvra, many times he made a request to Gladi to wear those.

Sou made special emphasis about her shoe – the Greecian style leather shoe.

The self guided missile – the Romance group had used some months before.

Against the nasty hole seller group.

The saints did not need these. They can defeat the enemies by prayer – Tou comments.

No one can defeat enemies by prayers to God. The value of work – the yoga of work – our work is everything. The universe is governed by some one who is called God – a mechanical system, you know. If you do good, the return will be good - Sou makes a lecture.

Cheaters never prosper, nature always take the revenge – Nou.

But we have to protest, we must not be a fool, or escapist, or weak – mentally or physically. If we support a evil, that machine will rotate in opposite direction – Sou explains the god.

So, we need these, Pou points to the missiles.

Yes, we can not seat idle, when others will attack. We have the action – Sou is positive.

The brilliant bees.

Yes, but probably, something have to add – Sou is thinking.

They are showing the recording – Dingi versus their gazettes, new to Bou.

Explicit enemy – the mathematical relation about the hs group from Bou.

How? Hou need explanation.

This guy is quite damn, Bou, in his mind. He wants to show his knowledge. Here the function is enemy and the relation is explicit you must understand the term explicit.

Hou nods in negative. Not in relation to human relation.

Suppose. Bou teaches – x loves y this much, Bou expand his hand to show the amount, and z loves y double of that …

Nou expands his hand doubly, this much?

Yes, then, how much x loves z? Bou put the problem.

X hates z – Pou makes the entry within love sphere. as no one likes a rival.

The hole seller group is not our enemy, we are not their, but those oppose them are friends of us, hence, explicitly, we also are the enemy of the hole seller group – Bou makes water the matter to Hou.

Chapter twenty five fantashe – 12

L L

L and L again – Sumansuvra push the L button of the pendant twice. The crystal sphere pendant – gift from Gladilova. At the time of good bye. Good bye from the earth. After their four weeks live together. The sphere has two buttons over it – two alphabets. M and L. Golden.

Sumansuvra is now at his planet. Far from Gladilova. He push the L button twice.

L before love – love is driving with L – learning – Nou solve the mystery quickly.

After such a long experience, driving with L? Pou is surprised.

Sou ends the dispute. No, no, it's simply latitude and longitude. Sumansuvra press the latitude and longitude of the position of Gladilova. Where she is just now.

Then? Bou wants the effect.

Gladi stands at the center. Not stand. That's not in literary sense. Gladi is viewed at the centre. Of the sphere. At her balcony. With her thoughts. Heaven and hell thoughts. Slices of memories.

Then? again Bou.

Then Sumnsuvra press the M button. And you see, a red rose band – single stripe from the rainbow surrounds Gladi.

And L L starts – joke from Tou.

All laugh together.

And red rose is a must there – Nou knows. Mou nod silently.

Specially a blackish red, my favourite – Tou expects that.

How Sumansvra fix the values? – Bou.

At that time? I don't know. But, it may be by touch, touch the lines over the sphere – horizontal and vertical, or may be some display.

The red strip is not visible to Sumansuvra. But he feels, that he is beside Gladi. Like the old days. He and Gladi sitting at the balcony. Sumansuvra continues to view. The sunset over the long eucalyptus – evening is coming silently, slowly, smoothly. The romance scene continues. This is their tea time. Evening tea.

Looking at Gladi, Sumansuvra ask – how are you Gladi? Gladi within sphere get a jerk.

Chapter twenty six fantashe – 13

A long drive

All around
Your smile floating over surround
All around

Gladi is at low decibel. A song of Sumansuvra. She is now examining the doors and windows. Of her farm house. Put the arm chair in its place.

No, no dust. All furniture are clean. Mary do her duty well.

Gladi left the balcony some minutes before. For her house works. The red band is now over the balcony. Matching with the red rose bush under the balcony. The common flower garden. For Gladi. Out of their business.

Gladi completes her cooking. But then, there is no engagement. Sewing? No. story book? No. Gladi's concentration now fails. She is feeling bore.

The curtains? They are in places. Not the time to change. Will she join Max? The office job? Or Mary? Who is boiling the eucalyptus leaves. After drying.

The strong odour is coming. Cough and cold quits from the farm.

Gladi takes out the necklace from the locker.

I am ready, she told herself. To Sumansuvra, actually.

Gladi suppress her anger. She is angry inside. Angry due to the fail. The last day tour. She knows about the vampire lady club. They never like her happiness. This is a long time fight. She heard, this vampire lady club members are like the witches. In nature. They never do any good for anyone. Very selfish type.

For the strong wind, she was forced to back from the mid path. Otherwise, she may reach Sumansuvra.

The distance – now she almost overcome that.

How much? Bou interrupt Sou. When almost all have drowned within the love tragedy of Gladi.

How much what? Love? Ask Sou. These boys are not growing up.

No, the distance – Bou wants to know the distance between Earth and Sumansuvra's residence.

From Neo to Iio or like that –Sou add over his draft. This is not the time of figures. Sou continues.

In anger, Gladi push M and L buttons without counting.

The farm is covered with two band. Orange and red rose.

Floating towards infinity – parallel.

Chapter twenty seven The Kathak

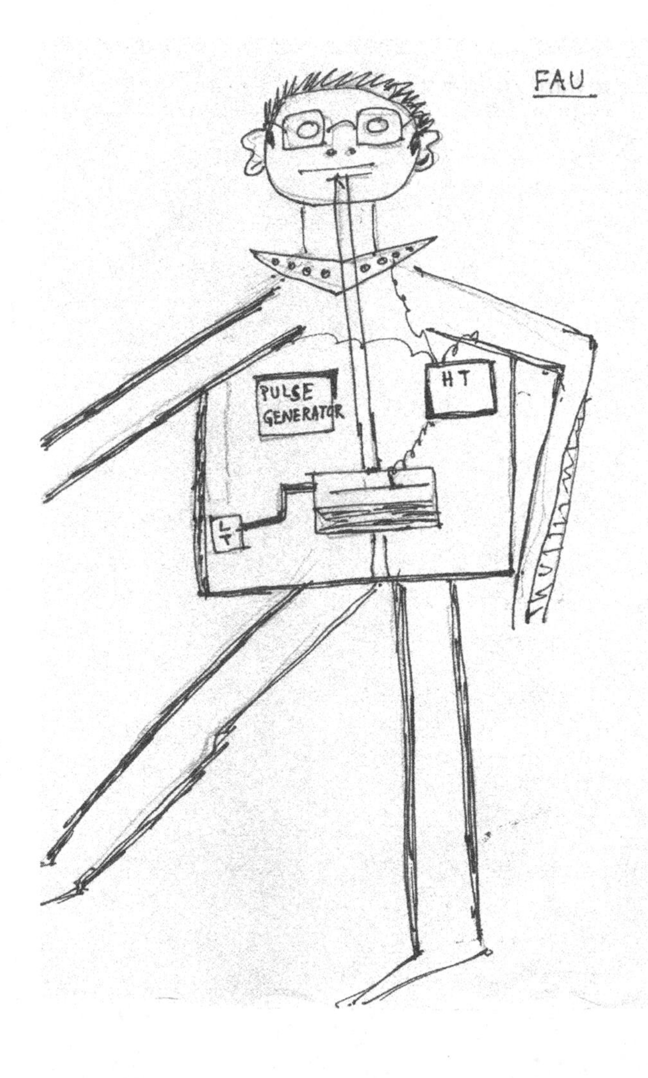

Sun ray. Now all the powered light are off. The white desert is full of sun ray.

Neo, the satellite of Jupiter has no axial rotation. No day or night. When it is within the umbra of Jupiter, always night is there. Now it is always day.

For its present position over the elliptic path of the Jupiter, Sun is at a distance. The sunlight is not so strong. But with the movement of Jupiter, temperature is increasing day by day.

And the expansion of the gas is in proportionate.

Uki is sitting at the center of the desert. Over its cave base. All white.

For last few days, some pebbles are at her lap and hand.

Pebbles like the beetle nuts in look.

The all over day is also divided in twelve hours. The clock necklace of Uki tells the day and night of both the groups.

It is the evening of Romance. The boys have returned from their work. All of them wait for this time. The time of relaxation. The time of fairy tale. The time of Gladilova and Sumansuvra.

Fau is not in the scene. He has not entered till now. He will be back when the power hunger will be strong. Now he will play with the Sampan boys.

Today they are dancing.

Beetle nut beetle nut
Cover my hat

Fau is dancing with Aayna Khayna Gayna. Aayna Khayna are not good dancer. They are moving.

Beetle nut beetle nut
Sit on my hat

The other are echoing to Fau.

Nou Pou Tou are at the window of Romance. They are watching the field and Fau.

Dha dhin dhin dha

Gayna add the 'tabla' tone.

Nou Toun Pou run to the field

To Fau.

Who is now in Kathak steps.

Chapter twenty eight — Heaven's gate

Earth is too crowdie. For long last time.

About five hundred years ago, at the starting of twenty first century, human beings land at Iio.

And built up the space colony. But, everything is artificial there. And have the capacity limit.

Now, the anchor is at Neo. But the hot and cold, both are beyond tolerance here.

The Sampan group, for last six month, make comb searching here for a residential place.

Following the Romance. Who got the 'rasa'(juice) trees, with the sweet juice. These can help to survive. But, the temperature. And the oxygen.

Matter is the population. Increasing day by day. And the pollution. Many one want to leave this dusty nasty world.

The Billa group. Connected to the Sampan. They have no wish to leave this Earth. They are happy here. But Iio people! Why they will be more happy. They have not to face the daily problems.

The Billa group wish to enter to Neo. To win over the Iio people.

The Billa group keep daily touch with the sampan. They must find out a space to stay. Out of the space sheep. Over the desert, under the sky!

Lastly they have found it.

The base of Uki.

Like the Troy of Hellen.

Not a large accommodation. but not bad.

It will be natural temperature controlled.

God always provide something.

The base of Uki will be their property. only the Romance boys. They must protest. Actually, Neo was their expedition.

So, the Billa must have a plan. Tthe whole matter is confidential. If the romance boys know by somehow, they will capture the cave.

The sampan boys are not so fit.

The gas. It must be made out of the cave. The Billa group decide to send some expert.

By hook or by crook they will enter within the cave. Brain and muscle, both power are required.

The Billa group get ready.

There must not be any late in good works.

Chapter twenty nine fantashe –13

I know these types of witch – Pou comments as the last line of the last day episode. At the starting of today.

I know, I know, Nou jumps, come to his memory - once upon a time, they forced one scientist to take poison.

Yes, I have heard also, those bad people were the servants of the witches – Tou supports Nou.

I know, they are still now, at modern time, they beat the scientists, to take away the money fame from them – Nou add.

And the poets, scientists keep silent – Bou, in surprise.

They must not let Gladi to meet Sumansuvra, they dislike other's happiness – Pou with the recent past. Gladilova and Sumansuvra are flying parallel together, but individual.

No, Sou brings the ending or the beginning.

How? Hou ask, they are separated.

By the clouds. The clouds over the mountain. Miles after miles. Gather there.

The witches done that?- Tou.

Yes. Clouds gather at the mountains, collide there, and come as rain over the ground. But those are small, with the borders.

Sou explains – this time they freeze to a big one.

Re crystallisation – Bou likes science.

But other is not in mood of learning. This time. Within the fantasy. So, they bypass the chapter of crystallisation. Specially the crystal from the colloids. Take granted that this is the work or bad work of the witches. Who oppose the chance to get a friend, to get a husband. They use their knowledge, their black knowledge.

Gladi and Sumansuvra are flying on a high – Nou comes out from the black.

Yes, but not they, the red and orange band. They are turned to bands by the magic crystals – gift of each other.

They are not seeing each other? Nou.

No, they are just flying, side by side, as a co incidence. Of the push of both.

Then? Pou.

A large cloud take entry within the bands – Sou with the main story.

That must be black – Bou have knowledge.

Yes, the rainy day cloud – Sou answer and then ask – why?

No, the bad people generally be black – Tou, with deep faith on good and evil.

No, there are many white villain also –Nou put objection.

Then?

Then the bands breaks. The orange band and red band separated.

Chapter thirty — The beetle nuts

But how all the beetle nuts fall there? – Nou and Bou are in the interruption. Sou leaves them for few minutes. Within the fantasy.

There means at the hands of Uki. A million dollar question. These are must be from some heavenly bodies. But why only there.

Others join. Sou is taking a little bit more time.

These are the fruits of the meteor shower, no one has any doubt about this point.

For last some days, these are on the hands of uki. The hands are on the lap lazily of the sitting Uki.

Meteor shower? Nou is thinking. But we have not visualize any light shower, he has doubt.

We were in sleep - Pou is sure.

But Aayna Bayna were working, at field – Nou.

The meteor shower are not always with light shower – Sou gives the theory.
The actual question is, why only there? At Uki's hand, he adds.

Fau enters. He needs a recharge.

Sou leaves others.

The power system is organic for Fau.

Those are for Fau – Bou laughs. They grant the affair between Fau and Uki.

Sou puts some yeast mixed vegetable to the stomach of Fau, through his mouth.

Those may be the parts of the hat of Uki – Tou, after his research.

But, suddenly her hat breaks? – Bou want more strong points.

Some times, the meteor shower, actually not shower, one large stone fall on earth – Pou comments.

They have heard it. never seen.

Fau's stomach is filled. Sou gives a pressure over the food. The organic matters burns to generate gas, to rotate a mini dynamo. The process is very old, but new for biobots.

Some gas comes out from Fau's outlet.

We must check the beetle nuts – how much they hard to crack – Nou.

The maximum thrust – Bou, with science.

Fau goes out. For the field. For Uki. On full charge.

Then, the long drive breaks – sou sit on the bed, with the link.

She found her at the poolside. over the poolside grass.

After some time, she came to form. remembers – she pushed the buttons many times. so that, she can move a long long distance. to sumansuvra.

But, now, she is here. where she was. at the earth ground.

It must be for 'g'. the third button. yes, it must be.

G or ji? pou ask sou. last time, there was lpji. not in the fantasy. but from the uki. in her voice. sou is very naughty.

No, g. the third button of the crystal pendant. with the necklace – gift from sumansuvra.

Gladi push the 'g' button. to check it.

Nothing happens. Nothing changes. everything remains as it was.

Then, it must be for some other cause.

She forgot the cloud? nou ask. he wish if he has an experience, to be a band.

The mass can not follow the wave – bou, in short. He will not share this. he heard, there will be question answer game at the end. the prizes, I need.

Sou also pays no attention. it is a fantasy. not a physics class.

Gladi returns to her bunglow slowly. everyone is now in sleep.

But, she is hungry now. she enters to her kitchen. something to prepare. for the diner.

At, the table, she is alone.

Chapter thirty one — The rounds

Beetle nut beetle nut
Make my wish full
Beetle nut beetle nut
Allow me to pull

Fou is dancing. Surrounded by the Sampan group.

Bou Nou Tou Hou ran from Romance. Reach within minute to them. Start their steps.

Nou, Nou, you and Hou are complementary. Yes, yes, perfect …Bou is the dance director.

And Tou, you and Nou are supplementary – it is the easy way to direct, through mathematics. Who will rotate in same direction, and who will in opposite.

Nou Tou Hou dance like that. In clockwise and in anti clockwise rotation. The main format of Kathak.

Allow me to pull

Fou gives a pause. the filler is ready by Gayna

Na dhin dhin dha
Tete dhin dhin dha

One of the Indian classical tabla tone. From the library. Others join Gayna.

Tete dhin dhin dha
Allow me to pull

Bayna is not dancing. Encouraging others, he poke his nose to the beetle nuts. The pebbles on the hand of Uki. Probably very precious.

From where these came? must be from the sky. Not only for jewellery value, but for research also – these are precious.

Bayna watch the fellows, and taking his decision – these must be in his possession.

Nou stop a while. Then change his direction. Fou is with the song. Keeping the rhythm.

Bayna, with his wrong steps, with the tone, now in double.

The hands of Uki are near to the base. Only Fau is at the base. Others are at the ground.

Bayna quickly set himself beside Fou. Fou ignore him. Lucky. Bayna pose like others. Move nearer to the hands, dancing style.

Spread his hands, as the pose, progress, to pick up some pebbles, Fou is now at his back, with the pose to pull.

But, success always keep distance from Bayna.

He is thrown off from the base.

Nou Pou Aayna Khayna. All stop their dancing.

Only Fau is continuing, spreading his hands, Kathak rotation, with four times angular velocity

Dhadhindhindha dhadhindhindha

His hand push Bayna, probably.

Natintinna natintinna

The oscillator – Bou, in his mind.

Na tin tin na na tin tin na

Aayna is managing - the speed – the circumstance.

Chapter thirty two fantashe – 14

Disgusting – Sumansuvra is disappointed. He was with the crystal sphere. To reach Gladi. Gladi was at the poolside. Their favourite place. Sumansuvra spreads his hands around Gladi. They were in that mood for a long time.

Suddenly Gladi vanishes. Suddenly Gladi vanishes. Sumansuvra moves back. But that was with a great sensation. Sumansuvra was feeling, Gladi is flying with him. It was like that journey when he and Gladi was towards the farm, from the sea beach cottage. Difference is that time he was driving. Gladi was on talk, about herself, about her family, about her likings, about her disliking.

Sumansuvra is passing his days with the thought – the future of them. Whether he will forget Gladi or he will be back. To the world. Sumansuvra is waiting for his decision – decision from his heart.

But their life need mathematics also.

They were flying. Towards the infinity. The damn clouds – coming down from the peaks. Their height of fly could not escape.

Sumansuvra was not made alert by Gladi – about the vampire lady club. He took the cloud as simple clouds. But, Sumansuvra noticed the clouds were not in folk – but was a solid mass.

The cloud – the damn cloud enters within them and break the link. Sumansuvra found himself at his own place. For few seconds, he require to update his position – the near past and the present. Then he looked at the sky. The sky of their planet.

A very thin line he found. Indigo coloured. Like the jet of smoke.

The colour is changing with distance. The indigo line becomes yellow line and then orange dot – at the furthest.

Sumansuvra remains sitting for a long hours. Very much confused. what is the direction of his life. He must find the answer soon, very soon.

My heart

Listens the echo of its beats

My heart

Is in resonance

Sumansuvra travels far with his song.

Chapter thirty three Billa company

They must not understand our intention. Firstly Neo and then Iio will be our – Billa group at the meeting.

But we must talk with them with honey filled words - member no. 1.

And we must be beside them – member no. 2,

Yes, what they want now? – member no. 3

What's their need in deed? –member no. 4

Garments, Iio is unable to supply the exact. They have send a request to earth people – no. 1.

Not to Billa, but to other earth person, Iio people has send request to send the cloth to beat the heat. At Iio, the atmosphere is artificial, wearing all time costume.

Actually, few hundred years back, we people designed the space suits, for the space expeditions – member no. 5.

Yes, but now they need summer cool uniform – no. 1. That is on process, for the boys' of Sampan and Romance. And also for Fou. He is also leaving the Penguin dress.

For the very mass of Neo, the citizens of Neo do not need any extra weight, the suits will be light.

And then, the costumes will land at Neo soon – member 4.

And the tailors – no. 1, some plan is flowing his brain nerves.

And we may send those for the Sampan boys 'only, the Romance boys' may suffer – no. 2.

The news of beetle nuts have already reach to the Billa group. must be precious – no. 1. We have to make friends with the Romance. L Last time the earth people had made some mistakes. This time, we, some modest sober type persons have to send.

Must be from the hat – no. 3. The beetle nuts must have fallen from the hat, during its lift up. He is speaking about Uki. The song brings the idea.

Fall due to the base rise – no. 4 supports.

The gas will expand more, as the temperature will increase. The statue will be shaken, and more pebbles will fall – no.1.

May be special gems – no. 5.

The Billa group is happy now, with the expectation. At last, they are earning something from Neo. For last one year, they are wasting time and money, gaining nothing. Rather, a big problem is created.

Time will cool the hot land.

Chapter thirty four — Costume

For the heat – Bou got the answer.

Beetle nut   beetle nut
Allow me to pull
Veil over face cool

Before the song reach at the last line, Bayna was thrown from the stage, only Fau as at the stage. Rotating with a high speed.

Bou, instantly detect the problem. For the heat, the operating point has shifted, the oscillator within Fou becomes faulty, the frequency has increased, Bou is thinking to stop fau.

Our oscillator is going all right, thank God - Bayna.

Like sudden start, Fau stops suddenly. Bayna's plan fail. He is unable to collect some beetle nut.

Matter is not so easy. I must wait for the Billa sub group – he promise to himself.

Bayna quickly changes his attitude, announced he has got the sample of costumes – summer costume for all of them.

For Fau also? – Nou ask. Fou is the dearest.

Yes, of course. All jump to the design of the costume.

The oxygen packets? – Aayna points. Due to the lack of oxygen out of the camps, the boys' need the oxygen packets with them. Their penguin dress also had the provision. Internally. Everyone's face was penguin then.

Tou quickly add two pockets for the packets, pipes will enter to their nose through the special hats, hats for protecting their head and eye.

Those are for Fau – Bou show the pocketless.

All will be same type, we will cut the pipes from the Fau's – Tou answer.

Bayna is silent. keeping other engage to the costume, he has returned to the incidence. How Fau had rotate with such a speed.

Aayna can read his face. Only, only, he knows the fact. He saw Pou over the stage for a moment. But he has not got the solution, what Pou did there.

Yes, Pou took some pebbles from the hand, rub them, and put on the hands – of Uki, where they were.

For that Fou makes the dhadhindhindha dance! Strange. But he will keep it in his mind. For the future.

Chapter thirty five Fantashe – 15

But spiders move on their feet, make the net for hunting, not to jump – Bou arise the question. Once upon a time, a spider man was a super man. Can move a long vertical height, or can jump from one high rise to another.

But the net formation can be done scientifically – Sou is with science.

How? – Hou.

By spraying some gel of high elasticity, no, plasticity – Sou's suggestion.

Pou Tou Nou are not interested in far past. The present is more interesting. Gladi and Sumansuvra are more romantic item. They requested Sou to back to present, to the fantasy.

To Sumansuvra, on other day, on free time. With crystal sphere – gift from Gladi. Last day, he had viewed an unnatural thing. A ray of band changing its colour with distance. He knew, this band is Gladi. For his gift. He knows the technology behind. Gladi was flying with him. He must take another chance. To be the side gladi. He makes himself busy with the LL – the latitude and longitude of Gladi. Yes, Gladi is at her farm. Thinking something. Today, he will view only – Sumansuvra determines.

Gladi is supervising the farm trees. Maximum of the plants are going to be fruitful – on of her favourite things to get. She waits to bloom the flower or the first fruit comes. Observe everyday, and notice, every plant. She becomes the happiest person when the first fruit is seen.

Being tired, she sit on the velvet grass, and then lie on it. The sky is over head. Sumansuvra get depressed. Probably, today Gladi will not fly, will not reach his planet, over his planet.

Gladi slowly regain her energy. her hand touches the necklace. slowly, her fingers move over G M L. Push the M and L, many times. she wishes to reach Sumansuvra. One orange band is over Mary and Max.

Sumansuvra find the band, flying above the sky, escaping the gravity.

But, God is not in favour of them now.

Rain. This time rain. Sumansuvra did not have the news of the vampire ladies. Have the black magic to send the storm or rain, if they need.

The orange band vanish. Gladi is bathing in rain within the kitchen garden, within the circle of apple trees.

Some one is calling me
    From the other side of the sky

Sumansuvra's composition is on her voice. Gladi is bathing within the rain. The rainbow arc is over her head.

Gladi is bathing is rain, within the crystal sphere, at Sumansuvra's hand. The rainbow is over her.

Sumansuvra got the rainbow.

The bgy – or – vi.

Blue green yellow orange red violet indigo.

Chapter thirty six **Nut shell**

Proverb or slogan, I will put on my costume – Bou,

My name - Nou.

Designers are on discussion. The dresses must bear the individuality.

The clothes have arrived. The Billa group also landed with those. The dress will be same for all, separate for Fou.

I will put my will here – Khayna shows the front of the summer jacket.

The power of attorney – Aayna.

Must be by name of that naughty guy – Gayna.

And must be signed by Bou, co sign by Nou – Bou add, to make the will legal, mathematically.

And tan for Khayna – Bayna.

The jackets are with insulation lining, very efficient insulation. The hat attached are also with insulation. Only the eye and lip are opened.

The Billa members have handover the dress. They already supervised the nuts. Almost handful now. Of uki.

The Billas call a party today. They are of small time guest. Will return on next day. Sampan and Romance, both camp is on holiday today. All are at the party. Even Jayna and Sou.

Beetle nut beetle nut
Make our wish full

The Billa members with Bayna have made a critical calculation. Bayna has found the time of the base rise. The time is almost fixed. As, now, the heat density remains same through out hours, the rate of gas expansion is also. Almost, at equal interval.

The nuts will fall from the hat of Uki that time, the Billas will collect them.

Sampan and Romance boys' have allowed the guests to dance over the base stage. Sou took Fou at ground. Fou is not happy.

Khayna Nou Hou Bou call Aayna at food tent. Food from the earth. Packets have just opened. A show with a smell.

A cry! A huge cry.

The guests are shouting. Their hair are straightened up with their hands. They are shaken. The Uki base is also shaken weakly.

Some nuts drop over the ground.

Chapter thirty seven Fantashe – 16

I must make a love – Bou is determined.

But your L shell is vacant, and electrons, I mean, future jump to M, direct marriage – prediction from Nou. They are influenced by Gladi and Sumansuvra's love story.

The Romance members are at the diner table. Except Sou. He is busy with the nuts.

Sampan boys' are at the field. Aayna and Gayna are with the guest. At the camp. Within the space vehicle. Aayna is on the cleaning. Of the labs and the rooms. His today's duty. He likes dusting. Gayna remains with him. To help him.

Bose – one plant specialist is recruited at Gladi's farm. Recently. Bose is taking classes. Gladi with Bohr Max and other workers are his student. Cardamoms will be collected now – Sou has started the bed time fantasy. About fanta(stic) she.

The big cardamoms are dipped in hot water – to prepare medicine. Gladi's business is now growing up. Bohr and Max transport the products to their city store. Bose feels the plants more than they. He stays at the farm. For supervision.

Gladi sit under the grape tree gate. She is now trying her best. To land on Sumansuvra's land. She is making the trial and error effect.

Yes, correct, I also, just going to advice that – Bou interrupt Sou. When the pendant knobs have no scale.

Right, sou appreciate. Gladi is changing the push of the buttons.

Today also, Gladi, after Bose's lecture, sat under the grape trees. With her pendant.

Sumansuvra was viewing Gladi. After hour, when Bose reach there, to discuss an urgent matter, he found, the sky has covered Gladi like a shawl. Bose nod his head. No, this is not the time. To break the blue shawl.

Within the blue shawl, Gladi push the M L buttons. Very carefully. She must not touch the G button. Last two days, unconsciously, she had done it. The days of rain and storm.

The orange band break the blue. Before the sight of Bose.

Sumansuvra view Gladi. Within the crystal sphere. Gladi has landed beside the fungi green sea water.

At the place where they met first. She and Sumansuvra.

But, today, Gladi is alone. Standing before their cottage. The crests and troughs welcome she. The boats on the cradles of ripples rocks, meeting Gladi after a long interval.

Chapter thirty eight QU

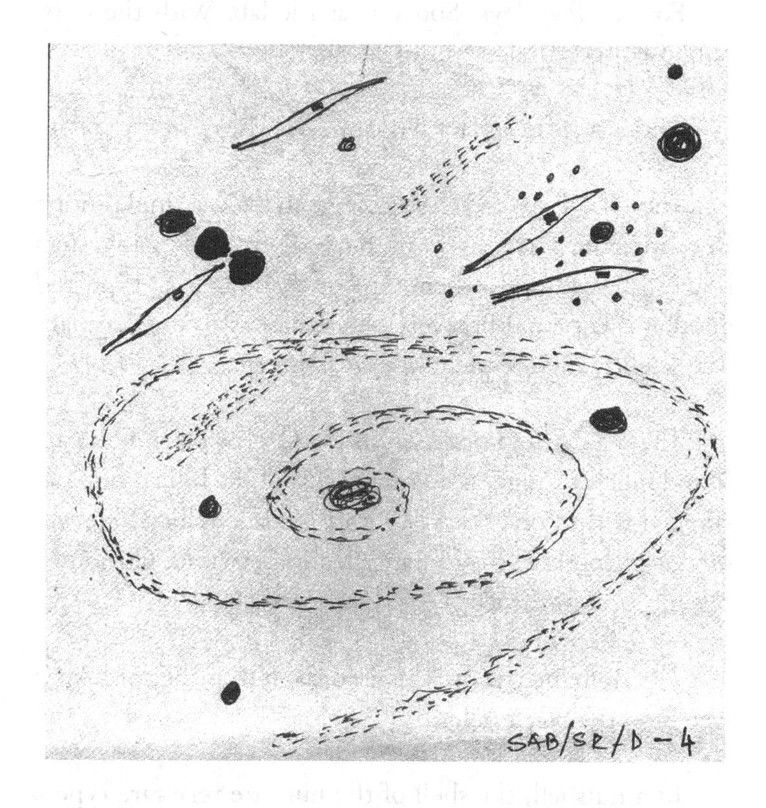

Not the heat, not the hat – Sou is the detective, to find out the origin of the beetle nuts. To find many other things.

I thought the oscillator frequency has changed, Fou has got double angular momentum – Bou with truth.

No – Sou make them cool. The circuits are not so fragile. That is due to the nuts.

For last few days, Sou was at the lab. With the nuts. Supposed to be fallen from Uki's hat.

And a surprising fact has came out.

The QU. Two black holes merge to make a single entity. Recently, the astrophysicists have discovered many such bodies. According to them, one of the hole is Q type and another is U type. But, everywhere these two comes as pair. The scientists name them in that manner.

The magnetic property of these Q type black holes are found much stronger than other. One of the Billa group has trapped within one such Q with his space vehicle. He was on duty to observe the romance from their head. Curiously, reach nearer to the Q.

The Romance team visualised the fall, as they also keep watch on the black holes.

In a nutshell, the shell of the nuts are very rare type – Sou has invented the fact.

The Q s and the U s are internally connected some how, scientists are at work over that. And till now, their statement is – we have found nothing except these two holes up and down, they are hollow and good for nothing. The great scientist Sanjib C. has declared the fact towards press.

It is also found, by them, the QU over Neo is more dangerous than other. It can capture five space vehicles at a time. Within its Q.

These are the gifts from the QU s – Sou show the nuts. Probably, as Uki's hat is at a larger height, the stones fall within it.

Like the feather of her hat – Nou.

Yah, the gas get heated, reasonably expand, the base is shaken, the nuts collide each other, and the static electricity generates at the shell, which can preserve it – Sou, with a single sigh.

And the oscillator of Fou's pulse is accelerated – Bou, lastly, the conclusion arrives, supporting him.

And Fou's hand throw Bayna - Pou,

And the next day, the Billa members, they theft the nuts from the hand Uki, took them at their hand. The static charges …

Within Sou's lecture, all laugh for the last scene, the hair of the Billa members ….

These are for Bayna – Sou wants to gift some nuts.

Chapter thirty nine Fantashe – 17

Gladi burst into tears. She is alone. Completely alone. She become angry with Sumansuvra. Over the beach, sitting over sand, over the shells colourful. And continue to cry.

One of the neighbour of the new city found her crying. He with his wife and children observe her from a distance. Gladi was telling the sea, if Sumansuvra has made his marriage within these days, she will give some slap, she will kill him. She sat till dusk. Till the water turn black, till the sky turn dark, and then returns towards the farm. Gladi's friend family did not found Gladi, after their walk, after their sunset view. Searching to return together.

Only a deep navy blue band over the blue sky was seen. Vanish! a living person vanishes before them. It is not realistic – it seems sur real to Sumansuvra's city neighbour friend. Or, it is the reality – he is confused.

Turns to ray, not a ghost – Nou want to help Gladi's neighbour.

But how? Hou, express at last, the major question. A man turns to ray band.

Why? Simply, by mass wave duality principle. Human body is just a mass. You can calculate the center of gravity of yourself - Bou has taken for granted from the initial.

That's correct, we can take, our body as the combination of particle masses, there are many such examples, Pou has strong support, the inertial rotation etc.

And the energy required? question from Tou's end.

All are silent. this is not clear to them.

Sou explain. the crystal have the property. To generate energy. And as these are god gifted, actually from other planets, may generate a strong force.

So, it may have a base, scientific base – Bou is satisfied.

Yes, Sou continues, when pressure is applied, the quartz always produce energy.

The electrical energy – Pou add.

And, Gladi gain it. Like the thrust by electric shock - Nou's hypothesis.

I have the experience – Hou. I was thrown about 4 feet.

It can throw 40 feet also, just a large voltage - Nou.

And also with a high speed, if God favour you, at the velocity of light – Bou.

Just you need to love one – Nou, advice.

And the 'my love'? I mean, the M and L? – he proceed.

Probably, those are, Sou tries, for the amount of energy generated that is, the pressure applied, and the wavelength of the wave.

Understand, the no. of push will change those two parameter - Bou makes it simple. Gladi will fly a long distance and with different colours.

Then it is a true wave, a love wave – Nou, but longitudinal or transverse.

Superposed - Sou is serious.

Chapter forty Problem

The walk through the imaginary axis halted temporarily.

A bad news.

The Billa group. News from Aayna Gayna. The Billa group is with some nuclear explosives.

Bayna is busy with QU details.

Aayna Khayna Gayna was with the nuts. With the nuts and the paper piece etc. Playing about the static electricity at the field. The Billa group was at rest, to their space vehicle.

Some how Khayna reach their, probably to ask their lunch menu, and their whisper enter to his ear. It was about some nuclear explosives. But, could not stay to hear the total. Due to fear. He quickly returns.

Sou is also listening. With other.

Well. This is the cause of their generousness - Pou. His words direct to the outfits. Within Romance, they are at normal dress. Sampan boys' have entered in their field dress. The summer cool.

Five hundred years ago, the explosives started their journey with the dynamites and reach to the LDX.

But now, the nuclear explosives are of maximum use. A very small amount is required to blow a large multi storied building. A mini edition of nuclear bomb.

What they want to do? Will try to destroy Romance with the boys like the last time? By the HS group. Sou thinks. But that need not any explosives.

Any how, we have to guard Uki. The Sampan boys agree with the Romance.

They are not happy with the Billa group. With their decision. with the problem at this peaceful land.

They have no merit of invention or creativity. always acquire from other, by hook or crook.

Like the vampire club – Nou, comparison with the fantasy. Just before the entrance of Aayna Khayna, they were drowned within the tale.

They decide their line of action. 'parallel to the x- axis, the real axis '– with a comment from Bou.

Will steal the explosives, when the Billa put at outside some place.

Bayna is passionate with his research. Luckily, he, thinks, there is none within the Billas who have any passion except money and power.

So, when, Aayna Khayna Gayna, inform him that all the research is just going to stop, Bayna makes the hand shake. He will, this time, against the Billa. The QU – he has got a storage of unknown, he has to solve those. There is the beetle nuts etc also.

No, no explosion at this high time.

The watch dog job starts. Very silently, very carefully.

Chapter forty one Fantashe – 18

That very day – Sou has just started.

Bou gives the connection 'superposed'.

After their war plan, Romance team returns to the fantasy. A half way of their a very well sleep.

Yes, but, that happened later. Before that, some days are gone. And today, it was a full moon day. The last few days, Gladi was busy at her farm, find a leisure today. Time to spent with 'G'.

Yes, G, the third button, of the necklace pendant. The effect of G has found by Gladi.

It is the 'ground'. the break of fly – Tou sounds, though others also got it. He listen the story with deep concentration.

These days, Gladi verify the buttons many times. Fly for a distance and land there.

And, now, she is ready – Sou, with the indication of the direction of his story.

And, today, it is a full moon day. Gladi wishes to prepare some special dish with the spices of her garden. Fresh, high quality. Strong smell.

She decides to call other. Gladi cook well. Bose appreciate all the dishes. Others also. A taste of their labour. They had a good appetite.

Without Sumansuvra – Hou is sad, in the absence of his hero.

No way, but there is a Chinese proverb, which tells – seeing is half eating. Sumansuvra take a half. As, he is, now, in keen observation on Gladi. He is intelligent. Last day, he found Gladi at the sea beach and on the return path – Sou is the speaker,

As the navy blue band – Tou, from his memory.

Yes, and he knows, that Gladi will try to land on his planet – Sou continues.

So what? – Nou, wants the landing.

Problem, the lady vampire club. They must send storm or cloud or rain or other obstacle. physical, natural.

May be the thunder, may be flood – Pou add.

Yes, and, Gladi is quite in the position that she is being unable to reach her destination. Sumansuvra, in between time, has collect the past history. About Gladi, about the vampire club. The cause of the change of path of Gladi.

The equation of motion will change for external forces – Bou, with dynamics. She will loose the energy at unknown point, may land to other planet.

Sou, after Bou's explanation, returns to the very day, actually night.

After the whole day program Gladi was very tired. And, she was satisfied also. For the success of the farm products, of the spices, of the cooking and also of the party.

Within the deep sleep, she felt herself inside of a buttery bath tub. For a second, she thought, it is the moon lit room, but her eyes found the faint reddish ray through the window spread over the floor at one side.

With the swimming in the melting butter, she spent her night.

Chapter forty two — Gas jet

Orange tub – Bou has explored the condition of Sumansuvra.

Gladi wake up from the butter tub, Sumansuvra wake up from the orange tub, and the days are passed.

The Romance boys are passing their days very carefully. And with the bands. The cherry red, strawberry shade, olive green, sea blue, sea green – separate on each day.

And the duty hours. All the time, they are expecting message from the Sampan. About the Billas. Pou Tou already, modestly, asked them – the cause of the halt. Why they are not returning to their home. Back to earth. They are avoiding the Romance boys.

The temperature has increased. The height of Uki also raised – the noticeable amount.

The Billas are happy. They will acquire the cave. The more will be the volume, more will be accommodated. They must win this match. the Romance and the Sampan groups will be back, the temperature is reaching beyond tolerance.

The toffee size nuclear bomb. Brought those from the earth. Just five hundred years ago, these gazettes were beyond imagination. The triggering mechanism takes a lot of time.

But, the Billas know, the Romance boys are keeping watch. A sharp watch.

Betle nut beetle nut
Allow me to pull
Veil over face cool

That element. Fou. Always near to uki. With the romance. With the sampan. Biobot must take a nap – the Billas wish. There is spy gazettes with it – the members are dead sure. Sou is not a fool.

And the nuts. With their electrical property. The Billas have the experience. Bayna is busy with those. They must move with awareness.

Plan after plan. But not satisfactory. Delay in taking action. But when there is a will, there is away!

Come to the brain of member 3. Toffee turns to nuts. The external get up.

Now, only to put up at the side of the cave.

The far sights are now all time busy.

Chapter forty three — Failure

The lenses of Romance. Set at the windows of the space vehicle. Mou, mainly, have the duty with those.

Aayna Khayna Gayna send the message. Of the colour change. Toffee to nuts.

We shall change those again – the easy solution from Nou.

The Billas dislike the friendship with the romance boys. They have engaged the sampan boys to other duties. Away from the romance boys.

But the message gets leak. Like the gas, through fine cracks over the cave. Due the expansion of the stones.

The Billas will put the toffee, as like the nuts, here and there, as they are fallen from the hands of Uki.

Sou team is ready. They will collect, as the Billas will shift. It is a common matter – they will trigger the toffee at their night. When the Romance will be at the field.

All the boys are at the windows. The Billas are proceeding towards Uki. Only a few centimetre distance.

A burst!

The Billas are blown. At different distances. Neither, they put the toffee. Nor, it is by the Romance.

Natural explosion.

A door has opened. The gas jet is spreading.

Probably, this is Fou's charisma – Aayna is in doubt. He has in his mind, the special style of Fou. The shake of his collar with stretching the leg.

And, Sou has put the cork in place – Khayna is in his support. They are now the viewer.

They hide it from us – Gayna.

Bayna, instantly ran to the place of operation.

But, not, the Romance have not hide anything. They will not collect the distrust.

It is due to the sudden temperature rise. Neo is now out of penumbra, totally. Sunlight is falling directly. The morning moon.

Uki!!- they come to sense.

The cave breaks, due to the gas expansion. But Uki is all right.

Uki is not wounded.

It is now on the ground. The base cave has destroyed.

With the gas masks, the boys reach Uki.

Fou is helping Uki to sit on the ground.

Allow me to pull

Sit on my hat

Fou's speaker has not changed its mood.

Make my wish full

Chapter forty four — Fantashe – 19

I don't like any interference – Sou is at a halt, due to the chatting about the explosion continues by Nou Tou.

Logarithmic – Bou explain to Tou.

But that is the only way – Sou starts again due to the others are eager. The climax. In last story, Sumansuvra and Gladi was departed, the story ended in tragedy. This time, their demand is comedy.

But how? – Hou's question.

That was the question of Sumansuvra, to himself, during the rides with Gladi. The storm the clouds the rain - to Sumansuvra, vampire club is not total clear.

But it goes beyond tolerance to live separated from Gladi.

Fou enters to Romance. Last night, the boys set Uki, over the desert shifting from Fou's lap. Without throne, Uki is not looking like before. But not a big difference. More close to the boys. And closer means dearer.

Fou likes it. Boys make a fence around Uki. Low height. And everything is as usual.

The wounded Billas are sent to earth, for medical treatment. Their space vehicle turns to ambulance. With Bayna as nurse.

Gladi is depressed also. Now, she has got the distance, direction and the ground. But the bad luck never leaves her. She has taken the truth her mind - she has to live alone.

Bose will be with the fertilisers. Mary with sweeping gazettes. Max and Bohr with the spices. And she has nothing to do almost. And after evening, she is completely alone. Only the recreation is the galaxy scope. Tune to sumansuvra.

Sou gives the brilliants to suggest something. For Sumansuvra and Gladilova. To show a path.

The God can end the vampires – Nou suggest.

No, God never do that, he can punish, but can not hang – Sou states the rule of the game.

By somehow, their plan can be suppressed from the vampire ladies – Pou, wise.

If, Gladi also had some arms, like those ladies, a machine over the machine – Tou, interrupted by Hou,

Like us, intelligent over automatic, matrix transpose over matrix,

Or spirituality over black power – Pou,

Or, grey matter over black matter – Sou starts, and that happened exactly.

Chapter forty five curtain drop

Sumansuvra's brain goes over the vampire ladies. Solution strikes there, Sou take a breadth, other are breadth less. Question at their face.

Interference – Sou announced, the only solution.

Interference of human beings, just imagine – Pou.

Sou, ignore, for the sake of the story, continues. Sumansuvra takes the final decision. Yes, now, no delay. Already, they have passed almost a year – earthen year. Gladi is about thirty two now.

And one fine morning, Max Bohr Mary found a black band over the farm. Lying over blue sky. They took it as the rain cloud,rain is coming.

The cloud expand beyond horizon, and then beyond atmosphere. The atmosphere is clear over the earth. No storm, no rain, no clouds.
Only, some places turns white, the roads, the roofs, the peaks.

Why black? Bou got the clue.

Two bands, one orange and one bottle green superpose, make a black – Sou, taking the stirring.

Sumansuvra push his M L button, when he found Gladi is also. For his planet, from the pool deck.

Sumansuvra, takes his U turn, from her side, with the buzzing

I take my victory lap
To heaven from earth

According to WIT (Web International Trust), Sumansuvra and Gladilova had landed on Sumansuvra's planet safely.

Sumansuvra, this time, help Gladi, to push G on correct time.

The boys are happy. Within their sleep, the song visit several times

I take my victory lap
To heaven from earth

To heaven from earth